LOOK FOR LADYBIRD IN PLANT CITY

Frances Lincoln
Children's Books

WELCOME TO
PLANT CITY

WHERE
PLANTS GROW
AND
LADYBIRDS HIDE

Look for the things in
CAPITAL LETTERS.
Can you find these things
in every scene, too?

- Ladybird
- Someone sleeping
- Someone crying
- Five grey mice
- Five bees

Daisy had a pet ladybird, who was a bit cheeky.

One day, Ladybird decided to play hide-and-seek with Daisy without telling her!

Daisy looked around, but she couldn't see Ladybird anywhere.

So she went to see Basil, the best detective in Plant City.

'Please can you help me find my ladybird?' she said.
'Of course!' said Basil. 'Tell me all about him.'

'Ladybird loves hiding,' said Daisy, 'but the city is so big and he is so tiny. I am worried that he's got lost!'

'What does Ladybird look like?' asked Basil.

'Small and red with black spots and a cheeky smile,' said Daisy.

Basil wrote everything down in his notebook.

CASE NOTES:
LADYBIRD LOST IN PLANT CITY
- RED WITH BLACK SPOTS
- CHEEKY
- GOOD AT HIDING
- COULD BE ANYWHERE

Basil picked up his magnifying glass...

...and gave Daisy a pair of binoculars.

'Let's look for Ladybird!' said Basil.

Daisy and Basil's first stop was Big Bones Primary School.
'Ladybird loves learning,' explained Daisy.

They saw an UPSIDE-DOWN RHINO, an ELEPHANT
BLOWING BUBBLES and a HIPPO EATING ICE CREAM,
but they couldn't find Ladybird. 'Let's try train station,' said Basil.

ART

SPORTS

LIBRARY

SCIENCE

THE TRAIN STATION

The train station was very busy. Everyone was rushing to different parts of town. 'I wonder if anyone has seen Ladybird?' said Daisy. But no one had time to help them look.

They noticed a TAXI FULL OF OWLS, a CAT SELLING TICKETS and a RABBIT WAVING FROM A CABLE CAR.

'Let's split up,' said Basil. 'We'll cover more ground that way.'

THE MUSEUM

Basil took a train to the museum. 'Maybe Ladybird likes ancient treasures,' he thought.

KING

FOSSIL

QUEEN

VASE

ROYAL DOGS

CASTLE

JAR

STATUE

IDOL

DO NOT TOUCH

DINO EGG

VERY OLD CUPS

BITS & BOBS

Basil explored the museum and discovered
TWELVE MASKED BURGLARS, a PAINTING
OF A PINEAPPLE and a GREEN SPOON,
but he did not find Ladybird.

SQUIRRELUS & SQUIRRUS
FOUNDERS OF OUR CITY

PLANT

EXTINCT
FISH

MAMMOTH
TOOTH

DINO
CLAW

DODO
EYE

COOKING
VESSELS

SEEDS, PIPS
AND STONES

DINO
POO

LYRE

OLD
BONE

ANCIENT TOOLS

ANCIENT
FLUTE

DO NOT
TOUCH

13

THE FUNFAIR

Daisy visited the funfair.
'Ladybird loves fast rides,' she
thought. She climbed up a tree
and used her binoculars to
look for him.

Daisy spotted a GREEN HIPPO ON A FERRIS WHEEL, a CROCODILE GOING DOWN A SLIDE and a DOG PUSHING A BUMPER CAR, but she couldn't see Ladybird.

15

THE RESTAURANTS

The two friends met up again for lunch. 'Ladybird must be hungry by now,' said Daisy.

NOODLE BITES

ROOT PIZZA

Basil looked closely at all the tasty dishes served at the restaurants. He found a SQUIRREL HOLDING TWO SLICES OF PIZZA, a BIRD FEEDING HER THREE BABIES and a RABBIT CARRYING SEVEN CUPS, but he couldn't see Ladybird anywhere. 'Maybe Ladybird wanted to have lunch with his friends at the plant nursery instead,' said Daisy.

PINE CONE CAFE

APHID JUICE BAR

THE PLANT NURSERY

The manager of the plant nursery showed Daisy around. 'This is where all of the plants in the city are grown,' he said. 'We love looking after them!' Daisy saw a HEDGEHOG WITH A WATERING CAN and a PIG WITH A PITCHFORK, but she couldn't see Ladybird.

WE ♥ FLOWERS

Basil searched for Ladybird in the greenhouse. He heard a BIRD SINGING A SONG and had a chat with a red-and-black-spotted caterpillar, but no one had seen Ladybird. 'Come to the rock concert later,' suggested the caterpillar. 'Ladybird likes music, doesn't he?'

THE CAVE CONCERT

The rock concert was held in the caves. Lights flashed on and off and everyone was dancing and having fun. Basil and Daisy joined in. 'You've got some cool moves!' Daisy yelled to Basil over the music.

The band was called the Screaming Bulbs. They dedicated their coolest songs to a SNAKE WEARING SUNGLASSES, a HEN PLAYING MARACAS and a FROG IN BOOTS. Basil and Daisy loved the music and dancing so much that they forgot to look for Ladybird.

21

HEDGE
HOSPITAL

MINT TEA

MEDICINES
&
HERBS

COUGHS

QUIET
ZONE

After the concert,
Basil and Daisy walked
to Hedge Hospital.
Through the windows
they saw doctors and
nurses caring for the
patients.

RESTING

HEADACHES

RECEPTION

A&E

ITCH CLINIC

BROKEN BONES

They went to the reception desk and asked, 'Has a ladybird come in today?' The receptionist checked the patient list. 'We've had a SNAKE WITH A BROKEN TAIL, a CHICKEN WITH SPOTS and a GORILLA WITH A RUNNY NOSE,' she replied. 'But there's no ladybird on my list.'

WAITING ROOM

DENTIST

THE RIVERBANK

'Ladybird loves sailing down the river,' said Daisy. 'Maybe he hopped onto a boat.'
She searched down by the water, and Basil climbed into the treetops
for a better view.

They met a CYCLING KOALA, a BIRD WITH A BALLOON and a SWIMMING SNAKE.
But no one had seen Ladybird. 'We're running out of places to look!' cried Daisy.
'Not quite,' said Basil. 'We haven't tried the market yet!'

THE MARKET

'Ladybird MUST be here,' said Daisy. 'We've looked everywhere else!' She and Basil visited every stall, asking the shopkeepers and customers whether they'd seen Ladybird.

COOL SPECS

FRESH & DRY NOODLES

FLOWERS

FAST WHEELS

FRUIT & VEG

They spotted a CATERPILLAR MUNCHING A LEAF, a WORM INSIDE A ROLLER SKATE and a SPIDER ON A BALLOON. But Ladybird was nowhere to be seen.

'I miss my pet,' said Daisy.
'I'm sorry we still haven't found him,' said Basil.
They decided to cheer themselves up by
trying on some silly hats.

TEA SETS

SILLY HATS

TRY THEM ON!

BOOKS & COMICS

27

'I'm so glad to see you!' said Daisy, giving Ladybird a big hug.
Ladybird smiled his cheeky smile.
'Thanks so much for helping me find him, Basil!' Daisy said.
'My pleasure!' said Basil.

'We're a good team, aren't we?' asked Daisy.
'We are!' agreed Basil. 'In fact, I've been thinking –
would you like to come and work in the
Detective Agency with me?'
'Yes please!' said Daisy, and they celebrated
with ice cream.

They were so busy eating that they didn't
notice Ladybird sneaking away again...